Published by Collins Educational
An imprint of HarperCollins*Publishers* Ltd
77-85 Fulham Palace Road
London W6 8JB

The HarperCollins website address is:
www.**fire**and**water**.com

© The Templar Company plc 1985
Letterland© was devised by and is the copyright of Lyn Wendon.

First published by Hamlyn Publishing 1985
Second edition published by Thomas Nelson and Sons Ltd 1989
This edition published 1996 by Collins Educational
Reprinted 1999

ISBN 0 00 303265 5

British Library Cataloguing in Publication Data
A catalogue record for this book is available from the British Library.

Printed by Printing Express Ltd, Hong Kong

LETTERLAND HOME LEARNING
HarperCollins publishes a wide range of Letterland early
learning books, video and audio tapes, puzzles and games.
For an information leaflet about Letterland or to order materials
call 0870 0100 441.

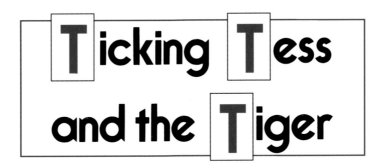

Ticking Tess and the Tiger

Written by Stephanie Laslett
Illustrated by Jane Launchbury

Collins

An imprint of HarperCollins*Publishers*

Ticking Tess was in a terrible temper. She had made a nice treacle tart and put it out to cool on a tray in the garden. But when she went back to get it, her beautiful tart had teeth marks in it!

From the tower Ticking Tess telephoned Clever Cat to tell her what had happened.
"That is very strange," said Clever Cat. "I left a lovely cream cake on the windowsill yesterday and someone took a bite out of it. The same thing happened to some buns Bouncy Ben baked — *and* to Dippy Duck's doughnuts. Whoever can it be?"

"I can't think," said Ticking Tess.

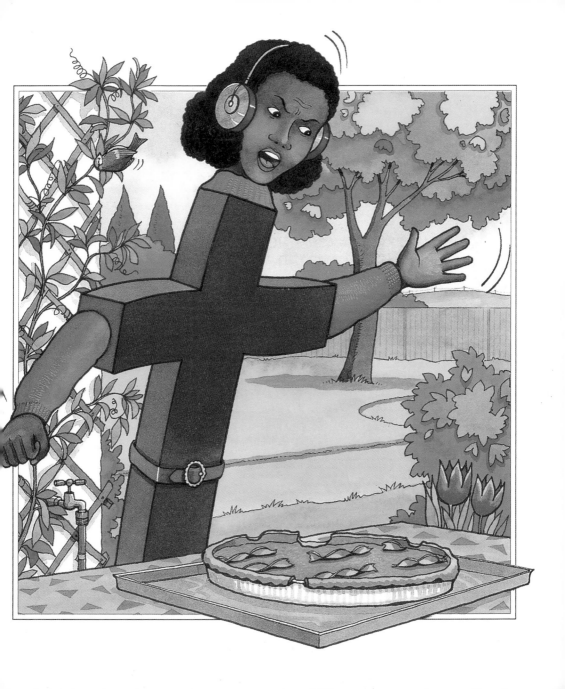

Ticking Tess put down the telephone. She was just starting to tidy up the Telecom Tower when a sudden noise made her jump.

It was her teletouch transmitter. "Ticker, ticker, ticker, ticker!" it went as it printed out a message.

"DANGER! BEWARE!" read Ticking Tess. "Escaped tiger loose in Letterland! Please tell all Letterlanders to take great care!"

Ticking Tess trembled. "A tiger on the loose! How terrible! I must telephone everyone at once and tell them the news."

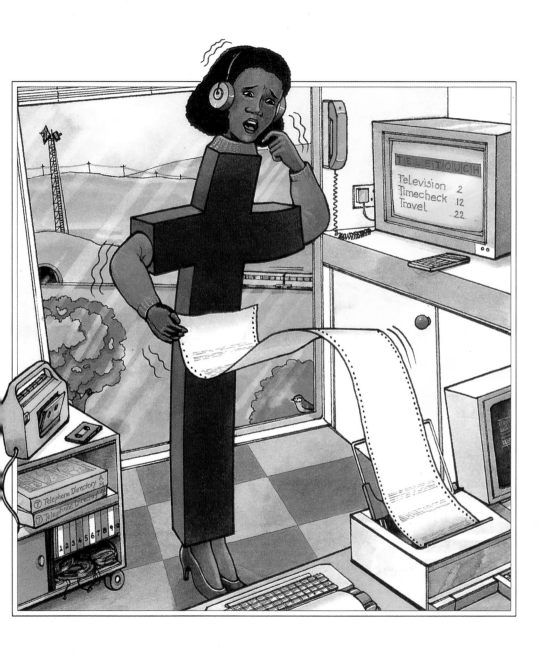

TELETOUCH

Television   2
Timecheck   12
Travel   22

Telephone Directory A-M
Telephone Directory
1 2 3 4 5 6 7 8 9 10

The first person Ticking Tess telephoned was her team mate Ticking Tom. He was setting up a new radar dish on a nearby tower block.

As Tess spoke she heard a loud roar outside and saw a stripy tail disappearing behind a tree. What's more, there was now a huge bite missing from her treacle tart.

"Oh dear! The tiger is here!" she said down the telephone to Ticking Tom. "Whatever shall I do?"
"I'll be there in two ticks," he said.

oon Ticking Tom arrived. Clever Cat and Bouncy Ben were with him.

"Don't worry," said Tom. "We have a plan to catch the tiger in a special trap. I have all the tools here to build one."

"Terrific!" said Ticking Tess. "But please don't build it *too* near the tower."

First Ticking Tom dug a huge hole. Then he stretched a tarpaulin over the top. Finally Bouncy Ben covered the tarpaulin with twigs.

"We need something tasty to tempt the tiger," said Clever Cat.

"How about some treacle tart!" said Ticking Tess. "I think this tiger may have a sweet tooth!"

All night long the four friends took turns keeping watch on the tiger trap. But Bouncy Ben was so tired that he fell asleep during his turn.

He woke with a start to the sound of birds singing. It was morning! "Wake up everyone!" he cried. "We must inspect the trap!"

Ticking Tom led the way as they all tiptoed to the bottom of the garden. There was something in the trap.

It didn't have stripes.
It didn't have whiskers.
And it certainly wasn't terrible…

"It's Todd Turtle!" cried Bouncy Ben. "What's going on?" muttered the turtle as they pulled him out. "I was just taking a stroll when I tripped into a trap … terrible shock … jolly tasty treacle, though."

Ticking Tom repaired the trap. This time Ticking Tess put some toffee in to tempt the tiger.

That afternoon the friends went inside to watch television. After a while they heard a loud noise. "Quick!" cried Clever Cat. Something was in the trap — and it was in a terrific temper. But it didn't sound like a tiger…

"**G**obble, gobble, gobble, gobble, squaaark!" it went. Timidly, Ticking Tess and her friends peered inside the trap.

"It's my friend, Terence Turkey," laughed Bouncy Ben as they lifted him out. "He lives on the farm."
"I am sorry," said Ticking Tess, but the turkey was so cross he could hardly talk.

"Are you *sure* you saw a tiger?" asked Clever Cat.
"Yes, of course I did!" replied Ticking Tess, looking hot and bothered.
"We'll try just one more time," said Clever Cat.

That night Ticking Tess had terrible dreams, full of tigers twirling their tails and twitching their whiskers. She could hear their terrifying roars in her sleep…

Suddenly, she was wide awake. She *could* hear a tiger! A screeching, growling sound — a terrible sound! Something was waving its tail through a hole in the trap. It had brown and yellow stripes. It was a tiger tail!

"Come quickly!" cried Ticking Tess. "We've caught the tiger!" They tiptoed down to the trap. Can you guess what they had caught?

It wasn't the tiger. It was Tabitha the tabby cat. She was in a terrible temper and they had to give her ten tasty fish titbits to cheer her up.

"Was it you who tasted my treacle tart?" asked Ticking Tess.
"Or my cream cake?" said Clever Cat.
"No, no, no!" cried Tabitha. "It was not me. I hate cake. I only like fish!"

"Well, who was it then?" cried Ticking Tom. But before anyone could answer a deep voice behind them growled,
"It was me, I'm afraid." And there behind them was the hugest, stripiest tiger they had ever seen.

"It's the tiger! It's the tiger!" they cried and ran away as fast as they could. All except for Ticking Tess who was too frightened even to move. But to her surprise, the tiger wasn't at all fierce.

"I'm truly sorry," he said timidly. "I thought you had left those tempting treats out for me."

"No, I did not!" cried Ticking Tess.

"How terrible!" said the tiger. "I would never have tasted them if I had known. To tell you the truth, I don't much like cakes anyway."

Ticking Tess burst out laughing and patted the tiger on the head.

"Don't worry," she said. "I'm sure I can find you something else to eat."

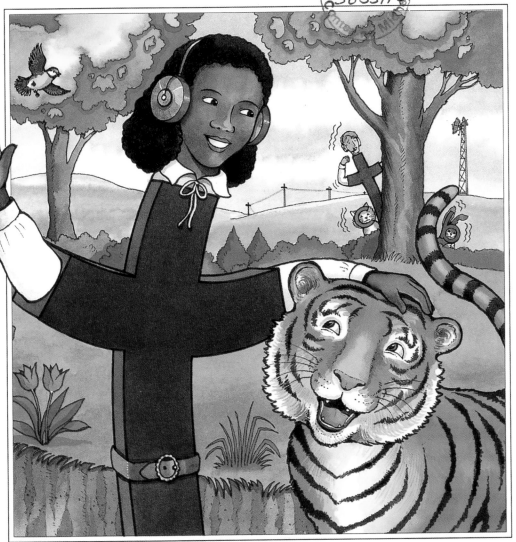

oon Ticking Tess and the tiger were sitting down to afternoon tea. Ticking Tess had tomato sandwiches and treacle tart. The tiger had some of Tabitha's fishy titbits. "Delicious!" he purred, popping one into his mouth.

Clever Cat, Ticking Tom and Bouncy Ben couldn't believe their eyes when they returned.
"Crumbs!" said Clever Cat. "Ticking Tess has tamed the tiger!"

And after that can you guess what they called Tess? Why, Ticking Tess the Tiger Tamer, of course.

THE END